Old Ben

Old Ben

JESSE STUART

Edited By
JAMES M. GIFFORD
and
CHUCK D. CHARLES

Illustrated By
RICHARD CUFFARI
Book Design By
PAMELA WISE GRAPHIC DESIGN

THE JESSE STUART FOUNDATION

Dedicated to
The Kentucky Jaycees

Old Ben

Text copyright © 1970 by Jesse Stuart
© 1991 by the Jesse Stuart Foundation
Illustrations copyright © 1970 by Dick Cuffari

Stuart, Jesse H., 1970.
    Old Ben / Jesse Stuart ; Edited by James M. Gifford and Chuck D. Charles ; illustrated by Richard Cuffari.
        p.   cm.
    Summary: When young Shan befriends a bull black snake, his Kentucky mountain family decides that perhaps the only good snake isn't a dead snake after all.
    ISBN 0-945084-22-6 : $10.00. -- ISBN 0-945084-23-4 (pbk.) :
    [1. Snakes--Fiction. 2. Mountain life--Fiction.] I. Gifford, James M. II. Charles, Chuck D. III. Cuffari, Richard, 1925-   ill.
IV. Title.
PZ7.S93701   1992
[Fic]--dc20   91-35578
                                                                CIP
                                                                 AC

Published By:
The Jesse Stuart Foundation
P.O. Box 391
Ashland, KY 41114
1997

Contents

Shan Makes a Friend

One summer morning Shan was walking barefoot along a path on his father's farm. There was nothing he liked better than going barefoot along this path the cows had made. He was going to the clover field where he knew a sweet apple tree grew. Usually Shan spent days like this with his cousin Ward, but today Ward had chores to do, and Shan had decided to see if the sweet apples were ripe.

If there were apples on the tree, he would climb it and sit on a branch and eat until he felt stuffed. Then he would throw the cores down for the ants and yellow jackets to finish. After he had eaten enough, he would fill his pockets with more for himself and Ward to eat later. Shan and Ward did everything together. They were both in the fifth grade at Plum Grove School, and they had walked in the woods together and played together as long as Shan could remember. They had even learned to swim, at the same time, in the Little Sandy River and to dive from a tree that leaned out over the deep water.

At the end of the path, Shan opened the gate and went into the clover field. The apple tree was filled with the fruit he and Ward loved, but suddenly Shan stopped short. Something made him look down at the ground. There at his bare feet, coiled up like the heavy strands of large black rope, lay a big bull black snake.

"Where did you come from?" Shan said with a tremble in his voice. "I almost stepped on you!"

The big snake drew its head back and stuck out its forked tongue to catch the sounds.

Shan stood very still. "You don't want trouble, do you?" he asked the big snake. "If you show any fight, I'll have to use that dead branch I see on the sweet apple. You're not poisonous like a rattle-snake or a copperhead, but my father says the only good snake is a dead snake."

The big snake kept its tongue out, catching the sound of Shan's words. It made no move to strike.

"I'd like to get friendly with you. But I've got to be careful," Shan told the snake as he slowly backed away and went to get a long, forked stick. Shan knew that even though black snakes weren't poisonous, they could give a person a bad bite.

When he had the stick, he came back to the spot where the old bull snake had been. It was still there, sunning itself in the clover.

"All right, big boy," Shan spoke quietly, "this isn't going to hurt." He slipped the fork over the snake, just in back of its head. The black snake flicked its tongue in and out and turned its head to watch Shan with its black-bead eyes. It looked very gentle lying there.

"Now," said Shan, collecting his courage, "I'm going to reach down and touch you. I have never touched a live snake before. But I think I want to know how you feel."

Shan reached down and cautiously put his hand around the snake's neck. Then he lifted it. The snake was longer than Shan was tall! Shan rubbed the snake's head gently, and then he stroked its back.

"Why the touch of you is good!" he said in surprise. "You're not what I thought you were at all. You are soft and gentle to touch. And you don't seem to mind me at all. You are the only black snake I ever touched, and I think my hands are the only ones that have ever touched you. Can we be friends? You are the first snake I ever wanted to be friends with."

While Shan stood there, he wondered what the snake would do if he put it on his shoulders and maybe around his neck. He was a little afraid to try. Did this black snake want to be friendly with him, Shan wondered, or was it just waiting for a chance to strike at him? Shan was strong and his hands were fast. So he thought, "Why shouldn't I take a chance?"

He wrapped the snake around his neck twice and laid the rest of it on his shoulder. And he wasn't afraid. The more he rubbed the snake's back and stroked its head the friendlier it became. It crawled down one arm and then turned and went back up to Shan's neck. The feel of it was nice.

Now the snake crawled down the other arm and turned and went back up to Shan's neck again. All the time it kept flicking its tongue out, testing the air for new sounds.

"I wouldn't kill you at all," Shan said. "You're real friendly. I'll come back for those sweet apples later. Right now I'm taking you home with me. I believe we are going to be real friends. And I know what I am going to call you, you friendly old snake. I'm going to call you Old Ben. Old Ben is a good name for you."

A New Home in the Cornbin

When Shan began walking toward the gate, the big black snake seemed content to ride on his shoulders. He was always in motion shifting from one shoulder to the other. Shan knew Old Ben could easily have slipped to the ground. So he was sure his new friend was enjoying the ride.

"Old Ben, you've never been carried before, have you?" Shan asked. "You've always had to crawl low on the ground and look up. Now you're riding up high where you can look down. Do you like it?"

Shan went through the gate and fastened it behind him. As he started walking along the cattle path toward home, he met Daisy, one of the cows who had strayed from the others. When Daisy saw Old Ben on Shan's shoulder she gave a loud bawl, switched her tail, and ran toward the herd.

"Don't you worry because Daisy didn't like you," Shan said. "She doesn't know you."

A Kentucky Cardinal flew down from a tree close to Shan's head and made a strange sound. Shan stopped and looked up into the tree from

which she had flown. There was a nest on a limb where four little birds were sticking their heads up crying for food.

"That was a mother cardinal, Old Ben," Shan said. "She was afraid of you. And she should have been afraid of you—because you eat birds. But don't worry, I know of something else for you to eat that you might like even better than young birds."

When Shan walked over a little hill and started down the other side, he saw Ward coming up the hill.

Ward stopped suddenly when he saw Old Ben on Shan's shoulders. He started backing down the hill and his lips trembled as if he was trying to

14

speak but couldn't.

"Don't be afraid, Ward," Shan called to him. "This is Old Ben. He's my new pet. He won't bother you!"

But Ward still couldn't speak.

"You wouldn't bother Ward, would you, Old Ben?" Shan said to the snake. Then he reached up and patted Old Ben on the head to show his cousin that this was a friendly snake.

Finally Ward got his voice back. "I came to borrow a plow," he said. "Aunt Sallie said you know where it is."

"It's over by the cornfield where we were plowing. I'll show you."

Ward still kept at a safe distance. "Where did you get him, Shan?" he asked. "Aren't you afraid he'll kill you?"

"I'm not afraid of him now," Shan said. "I found him out by the sweet apple, and he wants to be friendly. I never found any living wild thing in the woods or by the streams that walks, crawls, or flies as friendly as Old Ben is."

"You say he won't hurt me?"

"Of course he won't hurt you. Just walk up close to us and touch him."

Ward walked up closer. He put his hand up to touch Old Ben, but he drew it back. "Shan, I'm still afraid to touch him. I want to be friendly with him, but I never touched a snake in my life."

"Rub his back behind my neck," Shan said. "You know he can't bite you—his head is over on this side of me."

Then Ward put his hand on Old Ben's back.

"I've touched him!" he said. "I can't believe it, I've touched a snake."

Now the path was broader. Pine tree tops on either side came together overhead. Ward walked beside Shan and stroked Old Ben and patted his head.

"What are you going to do with him?" Ward asked. "You know Uncle Mick and Aunt Sallie won't let you take him into the house!"

"I have a place all picked out for Old Ben," Shan said. "I'll put him where he'll have plenty to eat. He won't have to crawl over the fields to find food. It will be a better home than he has ever had."

16

"Where?"

They had reached the barnlot, and Shan didn't answer. He just walked over to the cornbin, which was separate from the barn. He opened the door and took Old Ben down gently from his shoulders.

"Old Ben," he said, "this is going to be your home and I hope you won't ever want to leave it. There are lots of mice in that corn. We need the corn for our cows, horses, chickens, and hogs. You'd be helping us a lot by eating those mice."

"Where are your cats?" Ward asked.

"When we milk the cows, we feed the cats so much warm milk that they've gotten fat and lazy. They're so fat they can hardly walk. They won't even look at a mouse anymore. Mice-catching will be Old Ben's job now."

Shan put Old Ben down on the corn and stroked his head. Old Ben crawled until he found a hole and slid down between the big ears of corn and out of sight.

"This might be the last time you will ever see Old Ben," Ward said.

"No it won't," Shan told him. "I'm sure I'll see him again. Come on, I'll take you to the plow."

"When I get home," Ward said, "I'm going to talk to my father. I'm going to see if he'll let me catch a black snake, too."

Shan's Mother Meets Old Ben

After Ward had left with the plow Shan walked back to the house. His mother was in the front yard tying a rose vine to a trellis his father had just made for her. She was a tall woman, and Shan thought she was very pretty.

"Mother," Shan called to her, "you know what I have out in the cornbin?" There was a smile on his face. "You'll never guess. But I'll give you two guesses."

"You have some kind of wild animal that you plan to keep," his mother said. "Maybe you have a baby woodchuck!"

"Guess again, Mother," Shan said. "You're not even close."

"A young raccoon?" she asked.

"No, that's not it," he said. "I have a big black snake!"

His mother had smiled when she was guessing. She didn't smile now. "Where on earth did you get a snake?"

"Out in the clover patch by the sweet apple tree," he replied. "At first, I thought I would kill him.

"But he acted so friendly coiled up there and he didn't try to get away. So I reached down and picked him up!"

"You picked up a snake with your hands? Weren't you afraid?"

"I wasn't afraid after I touched him. Have you ever touched a living snake, Mother?"

"No, I haven't," she replied. "And I'm not about to. Why I'll be afraid to go near that cornbin."

"A snake doesn't feel as rough as everybody thinks. Touching Old Ben has the same soft feeling as wood moss and green clover when I walk over them with my bare feet."

"So you have this black snake named," his mother said. Now she smiled again in spite of herself.

"I call him Old Ben because he's a big old friendly snake," said Shan happily. "He's over six feet long."

"Six feet long!" his mother exclaimed. "How did you carry that snake home?"

"First I picked him up," Shan said. "Then I held him like a coiled rope. Then I put him twice around my neck and let the tail part of him rest on my shoulders. Then I took my hands off and he stayed up there!"

"Shan, that was foolish. I don't care how friendly you think this snake is. He might have killed you!"

"But I had it all figured out. I have fast hands and if he tried anything like that I would have pulled him off and killed him in a minute. But Old Ben didn't want to fight."

"Shan, I don't believe your father will let you keep that snake."

"I ought to go out to the cornbin and get Old Ben now and show you what a pet he is," Shan insisted. "But I don't think I'd find him. I think he's crawling among the corn ears getting himself a supper of mice."

"Leave him right where he is. He's as close as I want him."

"When you see Old Ben, Mother, just put your hand on him and pat his head," Shan said. "Then he'll be your friend too. I wish Ward had stayed to tell you about him. When he met us on the path, he was so scared he couldn't talk, but before we got to the barnlot he was patting Old Ben, too."

"Shan, it's a good thing your father didn't meet you coming into the barnlot with that snake around your neck. Have you any idea what he would have done?"

"I'm afraid he might have run up with his pocket knife and cut Old Ben in two," Shan said. "Please don't tell him about Old Ben tonight. Let him find out some other way."

"Don't worry, I won't tell your father," she said. "You'll have to tell him this story yourself."

Old Blackie

The next morning Shan woke at daybreak. He had been dreaming about Old Ben, and he was worried. When his father called him to put crushed corn in the cows' feed boxes, he was ready. As they went out with Old Blackie, the family's hunting dog, he was thinking how he would tell his father about Old Ben. Old Blackie trotted along quietly with them. He was a mountain cur with short black hair that was turning white. He had a big mouth and a big head, but he had lost some of his teeth. He was twelve years old.

When they reached the barnloft, before Shan could say anything, Old Blackie held his head high and began to sniff. Suddenly he ran for the cornbin and put his nose up in a crack between the planks. He began to bark and growl. Then he grabbed a plank and tried to tear it off.

"Stop that, Blackie!" Shan's father scolded in a loud voice. "What's the matter with you? You're supposed to be a great hunting dog and now you're barking at a mouse!"

"Blackie isn't barking at a mouse," Shan said

quickly. "Yesterday I put a big black snake in the cornbin."

"You did what?" his father said. He looked at Shan in disbelief. "Did you say you put a black snake in our cornbin?"

"Yes, I put my pet black snake in there yesterday," Shan said.

"Pet black snake! Have you lost your mind, Shan? I'll have to move a thousand bushels of corn to find that snake!"

Since they had come out very early, Shan's father carried a lantern. He was a big strong man, but now the lantern shook in his trembling hand.

"Your mother comes to the bin to get corn for the chickens. What if she sees that snake!"

"She won't be afraid of him," Shan said. "Once you know him, you and mother will love him."

"That's what you think, my son," his father said. "I feel just the same about a snake as Old Blackie feels. And you see how he likes one. Quit your barking and growling, Blackie! And stop tearing at that board. You'll break more of your teeth."

Old Blackie obeyed, but he didn't understand why he was being scolded when he smelled a snake in the cornbin. He tucked his tail between his legs and walked slowly back toward the house.

Shan's father opened the cornbin door. Old Ben was nowhere to be seen.

"Are you sure he's in here?" he asked. "Maybe he crawled out between the planks and left. Maybe Old Blackie was barking at a mouse."

"No, Father, Old Ben is back in the corn getting fat on mice. I don't believe he'll ever leave this cornbin."

"You have a lot of faith in that snake," his father said. "But every wild creature likes its own way of life. I can't believe a black snake is any different. A black snake likes to spend the warm days in the sun in the company of its own kind. On cold days, it wants to go under the ground to sleep."

"But, Father, no other wild creature I have ever tried to pet became so tame in such a short time," Shan said. "Everybody always wants to kill a black snake. The first thing they do when they see a black snake is pick up a stone or a club and beat it to death. They don't ever stop to think what a good friend a black snake can be."

Shan's father put his arm around Shan's shoulders. "I've always done that too, Shan, but maybe you're right. We'll talk about it later. Now we better get feed to the cows. Your mother will have breakfast ready before we get back."

A Snake At Work

Shan ate breakfast quickly and hurried back to the cornbin to find Old Ben. When he opened the door, there was his new friend lying coiled in circles. Old Ben's head was up. When he saw Shan, out came his tongue.

"Good morning, Old Ben," Shan said. "You know it's my voice, don't you?" He held his arm down for Old Ben to crawl up.

"Hurry up, Old Ben, get around my neck and over my shoulders. My mother and father are coming to milk the cows, and they don't believe what I've been telling them. I'm going to show them what a real pet you are. I want you to meet them because, when they know you, they'll be about the finest friends you ever had."

Just then Shan's mother and father came into the barnlot. They stopped suddenly and didn't speak. They acted just the way Ward had when he saw Old Ben around Shan's neck.

"Dangerous, my son," Shan's father said finally.

"Maybe I'd better call Old Blackie out here.

He would finish that snake in a hurry."

"Don't, Father!" Shan said. "See what a pet he is. He won't get down off my shoulders until I put him down. He likes it up here!"

"Do you know, Mick, I believe he is a pet," Shan's mother said in wonder.

"Whoever heard of a pet black snake?" Shan's father asked. "What came over you to pick up a black snake when there are so many other things that you could find for a pet? It isn't natural."

As he talked, Shan's father walked up closer to Shan and Old Ben. "That's a very old bull black snake," he said. "What do you plan to feed him? He's big enough to swallow a half-grown rabbit. It will take a lot to feed that snake, as big as he is."

"You know a snake likes mice, Father, and the mice are eating up the corn in the bin. Look how full and happy Old Ben looks! I know he's had a good meal on mice already."

"Well it might be a good idea to leave him here to catch the mice at that—if he'll stay," his father said. "We lose eighty bushels of corn a year in that bin. And I do keep my cats too fat."

"Mick," Shan's mother said, "I want you to let Shan keep Old Ben."

"That's just what I'm thinking of doing. If that snake doesn't eat all the mice in the cornbin, he'll scare them out. But, Shan, I won't be responsible for what happens to him if he gets out in the barnlot."

"He'll stay in the cornbin," Shan said. "Maybe we can give him a little milk every day, too. I read that snakes in the zoo drink milk. With mice to eat

30

and warm milk to drink, I know he'll stay here."

"All right," his father said, "we'll try it and see what happens."

"Father, you've made me so happy!" Shan said. "And I know Old Ben is happy, too." Shan put his hand on Old Ben's head and stroked him.

Shan''s mother stepped backward. "Do you really trust him, son?"

"I trust him," Shan replied. "Why don't you come closer and touch him like Ward did? He's looking the other way now."

Slowly Shan's mother stepped closer and slowly reached out to touch Old Ben's back with the tips of her fingers.

"Why he's as soft as a new-washed cotton dress before it's ironed!" she said. "Mick, just touch Old Ben once."

"I don't like to touch a snake," he said. "But since you have, Sallie, when he gets his head turned from me I'll touch him too."

Shan's father touched Old Ben with his big rough hand. "You're right—his skin really is soft. It's as soft as warm water! I'm not afraid of him now, son," he said. "Put him across my shoulder if you want to. I won't hurt him unless he tries to hurt me."

"He's not going to hurt you," Shan said. He laid Old Ben on his father's shoulders. When Old Ben crawled around his father's sunburned neck, Shan and his mother laughed.

"You want me to take him down now, Father?"

"He feels so nice crawling around my neck I'd

like to keep him there, but I do have work to do. I don't have time to play with your Old Ben now, but I think we're going to be friends."

Shan lifted Old Ben down and let him slide like a soft rope through his hands onto the floor.

"I know there's an extra pan," Shan's mother said. "When we finish milking, we'll fill it with warm milk for him. I don't want him outside the cornbin. He might scare the chickens and cows."

"He might scare them now. But just give Old Ben time, and he'll make friends with them," Shan said. "They'll soon learn Old Ben is a friendly snake. Everybody and every living thing around this barn except the birds will love Old Ben."

"Old Blackie can learn, I guess," his father said, "and maybe the horses in time. But not the hogs. You know what hogs will do to a snake, don't you?"

"No, I don't," said Shan.

"They'll stomp him and eat him," his father said.

"I didn't know that about hogs," Shan said. "But the lot for our hogs is down below the barn. Old Ben won't be going down there. If he ever wants a drink of water, he's close to the barn. And if we give him milk night and morning he won't even need to go looking for water."

"I hope you're right," his father said. "Now let him go back into the corn. We have work to do and so does Old Ben."

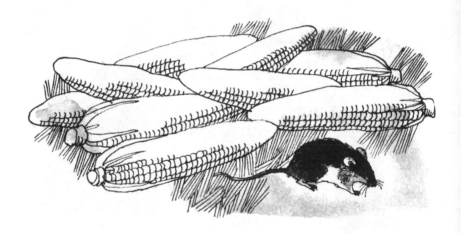

Unlikely Friends

Every morning Shan helped his mother and father with the milking. Their twelve cows gave over forty gallons of milk night and morning. When the milking was done and the cats had been fed, Shan and his mother carried the buckets to the milkhouse. Shan turned the separator while his mother poured the strained milk into it. Then he carried the cream in cans to the place where it would be picked up by a truck and hauled to the creamery. Meanwhile, Shan's father carried the skimmed milk to the hog lot and poured it into troughs for the hogs. They squealed and rammed the sides of their pen each morning until they got their warm skimmed milk.

Now, each morning, Shan took milk to Old Ben, too. Every evening the milk was gone, and the pan had to be refilled. Old Ben was busy a good part of the day hunting mice in the corn, but often he was curled up sleeping on an old burlap sack Shan's mother had brought him for a bed.

One morning Shan had an idea. When the chores were done and his father had gone down to the hog pen, Shan took Old Blackie to the house and locked him in a bedroom. Then he hurried back to the cornbin.

When he opened the door Old Ben was wide awake and ready to climb up Shan's arm.

"Not this morning," Shan told him. "Today I want you on the ground in your own world. I want you to follow me like Old Blackie follows us. I'll be very happy if you learn to follow me!"

Shan opened the cornbin door and moved forward quickly to keep Old Ben from trying to climb up his leg and around his body to his shoulders.

When Shan moved forward, Old Ben began to crawl behind him. He held his head high looking to his right and left and straight ahead. As they moved out of the barnlot and along the path, Old Ben left his track behind him. It was a smooth, crooked mark about an inch wide. Only when Old Ben moved on the green grass near the house did the trail disappear. Old Ben was down in his own world, but he followed Shan.

Just as they reached the front gate, Shan's father came around the corner of the house. He did not see Old Ben until Shan opened the gate.

Then he cried out, "Shan, what are you thinking of, bringing Old Ben here? He should stay in the cornbin where he's safe!"

"It's all right, Father. Blackie is locked in my bedroom. I fastened him up when you were carrying skimmed milk to the hogs."

"I'm certainly glad of that," his father said with

relief. "Now that you've brought Old Ben here, maybe we'll give Old Blackie his first lesson in not killing black snakes. Pick Old Ben up and give him to me."

Shan reached down and lifted Old Ben up. Then he laid him over his father's shoulders.

"Good," his father said, smiling. "Now go let Old Blackie out."

"Father, I'm afraid to let him out and you with Old Ben around your neck. You know how high Old Blackie can jump!"

"I'll talk to Old Blackie," his father said. "Go let him out."

Shan obeyed his father. He went to his room and opened the door. Old Blackie was so glad to get out he jumped up and kissed Shan's face with his long red tongue.

"Easy, Blackie," Shan said. "Easy. Not so fast."

But Old Blackie went running through the house toward the door. When he reached the screen door he charged against it.

"Easy, Blackie, easy, easy now," Shan's father said in a loud voice.

Old Blackie looked up and saw the snake on his master's shoulder. He began to bark.

"Quiet, Blackie," Shan's father said. "Quiet! No barking!"

Shan had arrived behind Old Blackie and threw his arms around the dog's neck.

"Don't hold him, Shan," his father said. "Open the door and let him out! Old Blackie has to meet Old Ben!"

"I'm afraid, Father. He'll jump up and grab Old Ben," Shan said. "Old Blackie will finish him if he ever gets him in his mouth."

"I'll see to it that he doesn't get Old Ben," his father said.

Shan opened the door and held his hands over his face. He was sure Old Ben would be killed. Old Blackie rushed out the door barking and growling and leaped up to get the black snake from his master's shoulder.

"I told you," Shan said. He took his hands from his face. "I told you."

His father reached with his big hand and pushed Blackie backward. Old Blackie hit the ground hard. He couldn't understand this treatment. He got up and stood looking at his master with sorrow in his big black eyes.

"I told you to be easy, Blackie," Shan's father said. "I told you no. Old Ben is our friend and you're our friend. And we want you to leave Old Ben alone!"

Old Blackie was a very sad dog. He couldn't understand.

"Come up here, Blackie," Shan's father said. "I want you to touch lips with Old Ben. I want you to know your friend better."

When his master reached up and lifted Old Ben down and held him in his arms, Blackie watched. After he had been shoved back once with his master's hand he didn't attempt to make another wild leap. He stood there looking up at the snake. Shan's father held the snake in his big arms against his body to protect it from his dog. He held its neck in his hand. Gently he put the snake's head out toward Blackie.

"Easy, easy, Blackie," he said softly. "Don't bite."

Blackie could not have bitten Old Ben without biting his master's hand. He stood very still while Mick put Old Ben's hard lips up to Blackie's. Old Ben squirmed for he knew most dogs were his enemies. Blackie didn't like the feel of the snake's hard lips, but he didn't move.

"Father, you did just right," Shan said. "Now, Blackie knows you don't want him to kill Old Ben."

"It will still take some time before Blackie learns never to bother Old Ben," his father said. "But Blackie is a smart dog."

Then he put Old Ben in Shan's hands.

"Take him back to the cornbin," his father said. "He'll need a little rest in his own home."

Shan walked along the path toward the barn with Old Ben wrapped around his arm. He didn't put him down on the ground to follow. He was afraid Blackie might come running to get him.

A Member of the Family

As the weeks progressed, Old Ben became a member of the family. Every day, Shan and his mother and his father went to the cornbin to see him and bring him fresh milk. Even Blackie had come to accept him. Ward came almost every day, too. "I'm looking for a pet black snake all the time," he told Shan. "I've talked to my father about it. Now that I know Old Ben I'm not afraid of black snakes."

Afternoons when Shan went to bring the cows home he often took Old Ben with him. He would carry his pet until they found the cows and then let him crawl all the way back home. He knew Old Ben needed exercise, and he thought Old Ben would like to hear the summer sounds over the pasture fields and feel the cool wind blowing over his long body as he crawled through the green grass.

A wonderful thing had happened. Now not a cow in the herd was afraid of Old Ben. They had seen him so often riding on Shan's shoulders that they no longer ran from him. Once Daisy came up and stuck her nose close to Old Ben on Shan's shoulder. When she sniffed and made a loud sound

Old Ben was more scared than she was.

One afternoon when the cows had wandered to the far side of the pasture to the shade of the willows, Shan had to go in the direction of the clover path where he first met Old Ben. This time he did not put his pet down on the ground.

"Old Ben," he said, "I believe you know this path. If I were to put you down here I wonder if you would crawl away and leave me. You're getting heavy and you're warm around my neck, but I'm going to carry you."

That day as he put Old Ben back in the cornbin he said, "You're really going to stay, aren't you? You love your home and you love me and I love you." Old Ben slid to the floor and disappeared in the corn. Shan was sure he was content with his home.

As Shan came out of the cornbin, he saw his mother and father talking to Ward in the barnlot. Ward was very excited.

"Ward has found something," Shan's mother said. "Let's go see what it is."

"It's up on the sandstone cliff," Ward said. "I'm not sure what it is."

Everyone followed Ward up the barnyard slope to the cliff. Near the top Ward stopped.

"There," he said, pointing to a spot where he had been digging. "There's a nest of eggs in the hole." On the ground near the hole was a very white egg. Shan reached down and picked it up.

"What is it?" he asked.

"There are six more in there," Ward said.

"Don't either of you know what that is?" Shan's father asked. "I'm surprised. You two know so much about all the wildlife around here. That's a black snake's nest!"

"Black snake!" Ward cried.

"I didn't know they laid eggs," Shan said.

"The rattlesnake and the copperhead have their young like a cow has her calf," his father said, "but a black snake lays eggs."

"And, boys," Shan's mother said, "look what a nice place this old mother black snake has chosen. Here in the dry, warm sand where the sun hits. The sun warms the sand, and this hatches the eggs."

"Everything is according to its nature," Shan's father said. "Everything that walks, flies, or crawls has its own way of life. Ward, put the egg back in the warm sand and cover the nest over."

"Uncle Mick, maybe Old Ben has a wife out here some place," Ward said.

"Do you think he could, Father?" Shan asked.

"Well I hadn't thought of that, but he could have. I've been noticing tracks around the cornbin lately. I think he's getting out—maybe at night. Snakes do travel at night."

"I don't care if he goes out at night," Shan said, "just as long as he comes back."

"It worries me just the same," his father said. "I'll have to bring the horses in soon and they don't know Old Ben. And I don't want him to stray toward that hog lot!"

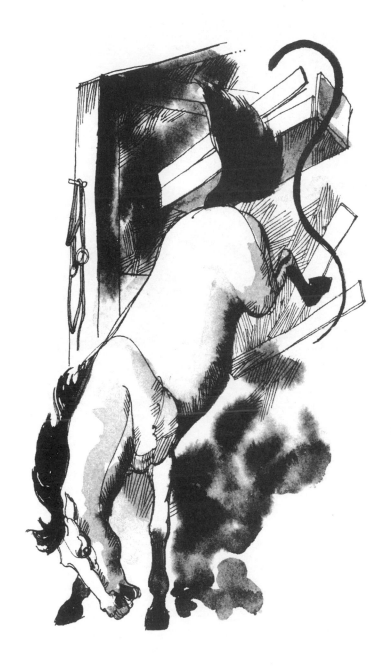

Asleep in the Feedbox

Late in August, Shan's father brought the horses, Old Kate and Old Fred, back to their barnstalls. "They have hard work to do," he told Shan. "They need to be fed corn. Watch over Old Ben. See that he doesn't get out in the barnlot. I don't want him spooking the horses."

"If Old Kate and Old Fred knew Old Ben, they'd like him," Shan said.

"Old Ben is too friendly with everything," his father said.

On the third day after the horses had returned, Shan took them out to the waterhole to let them drink. He rode Old Fred back and led Old Kate. When they reached the barn, he dismounted and pulled Old Fred's bridle off and let him go back into his stall. Then he removed Old Kate's bridle. She followed Old Fred into the barn and went to her stall. As Shan began to close the barn door, the horse put his nose down into his feed box.

Suddenly Old Fred jumped so high his head hit the barnloft. He let out a wild snort. Then he turned around in his stall and began kicking the feed box. Old Fred was wilder than Shan had ever seen him. As Shan watched, he kicked the feed box loose from the manger. The feed box flew up into the air and out of it tumbled Old Ben. As soon as Old Ben hit the floor he began crawling away in a hurry. Old Fred came out of the barn door past Shan and ran a circle in the barnloft, snorting every breath.

Shan watched in horror. But Old Ben ran on the ground like a black streak and headed for the cornbin. He lifted his head and then his long body up the outside wall of the bin. His head went through a crack between the boards and his long body followed.

Shan ran back to the house to tell his father what had happened.

"Until I turn the horses back into their pasture, Old Ben better stay out of that barn," his father said. "They'll stomp him to death if they catch him."

"Old Ben can run fast, Father. When that box went up in the air, Old Ben went higher. As soon as he hit the barn floor, he was running. They wouldn't have caught him."

"Shan, one of the horses could pick Old Ben up on the ground in a very short distance. I don't care how fast he can run. A horse is faster than a snake. I think I know now why Old Ben is getting out of the cornbin."

"Why is he?" Shan asked.

"You know, son, we don't hear mice in the corn any more. Old Ben has caught them all. He's going into the hay in the barn loft hunting for more.

When a snake gets a big meal he wants to take a nap afterwards. On a hot day like this Old Fred's feed box seemed like a nice place to coil up in and go to sleep."

"What are we going to do, Father?" Shan asked. "I don't want Old Ben killed."

"I don't either," his father said. "That snake has saved me hundreds of dollars this summer. Mice destroy a lot of corn. And mice can do damage in hay. When our cows smell hay a mouse has been in, they won't eat it. Maybe we should never have put Old Ben to work for us, but now I am going to let him clear out the barnlot. I'll take the horses back to their pasture. I'll wait until October to haul the logs."

"Good," Shan said. "By that time Old Ben will have found himself a place to sleep for the winter."

51

Old Ben Disappears

August passed and September came. Old Ben spent the days in the cornbin or in the barn. He still went with Shan to bring the cows home. Unless he was sleeping in the cornbin or hiding under the hay, someone was playing with him all the time. The days were still very warm, but the nights were getting colder. It was almost time for the first frost. Sometimes now Old Ben seemed very sleepy. Shan knew that before long he would be looking for a place to spend the winter. Cool weather chilled the blood in a snake and made him sleepy. It was nature's warning to him that October frosts and November rains and snow were coming.

On the last day of September, when Shan poured milk into Old Ben's pan, Old Ben was nowhere to be seen. "He must be in the hayloft," Shan said to himself. "Wherever he is, he'll be back for his milk."

But when Shan stopped at the cornbin in the afternoon, the milk was still in the pan. "I wonder where he is?" Shan said aloud.

The next day Old Ben still had not returned.

Shan's mother poured the old milk from his pan and refilled it with fresh. The third, fourth, fifth, and sixth days passed, and Old Ben had not returned.

"He's been away a long time, Mother," Shan said. "Something may have happened to him."

"Old Ben can do without water or milk for a few days," his mother said, "but he will surely have to come back tonight or tomorrow morning."

"Maybe he has found a place to sleep for the winter," Shan said.

"It's getting late in the year all right," his father said, "but I think the days are still too warm. I think we'll find him full of mice and asleep up there in the hay. If he doesn't come back tomorrow, we'll throw the hay down from the barnloft and hunt for him."

The next morning Shan hurried out to the cornbin. Old Ben's pan of milk was there and beside it was his empty burlap sack. Old Ben had not come home.

"Old Ben's not here," Shan told his father.

"Then after the work is done this morning we'll fork the hay down from the loft," his father said.

After they had milked, separated the cream, and fed the hogs, Shan and his father went up into the barn loft. They each took a pitchfork and began to fork the hay down into the large stalls of Old Fred and Old Kate.

"Look closely for Old Ben, Shan," his father said. "You might stick him with the pitchfork."

"I'm being careful," Shan said.

When they had thrown most of the hay down

they had empty space in the loft. Now they began to fork hay over onto the clear floor. The work went faster. Soon all the hay had been turned.

"Well he isn't here," Shan said.

"I haven't seen a mouse," his father said. "He's cleaned them all out of the hay, just like he cleaned them out of the corn."

"Do you suppose, Father, he's gone somewhere to hunt for more mice?"

"I'm puzzled about Old Ben now," his father replied. "I don't know what to think."

They had worked until noon. Now they went into the house to eat lunch.

"Did you find any sign of Old Ben?" Shan's mother asked.

"No, we didn't," Shan said.

"I just can't believe he would leave us," his mother said.

"Shan and I will have to fork the hay into the loft again," said his father. "Maybe you can help us hunt, after you finish the dishes."

"And, Mother, if Ward comes, send him out. Ward knows a lot about Old Ben."

"We'll all be out there helping you look for Old Ben," his mother said. "He must be around the barn some place."

What Happened to Old Ben?

For the next hour Shan and his father worked to replace the hay. His father threw forks full of hay up into the loft, and Shan spread it around.

Shan's mother joined them and was looking in the mangers of each horse stall. When Ward arrived, he began searching for tracks around the cornbin and the barn.

At last Shan and his father put their pitchforks away in the loft and walked down the steps and out the barn door.

"Old Ben is not here," Shan's mother said. "There isn't a place we haven't searched."

Just then Ward came from behind the barn. "I think I found Old Ben's track," he said.

"Old Ben wouldn't have gone down the backside of the barn!" Shan said.

"It's old, but it looks like a track," Ward said.

"It won't hurt to see what Ward has found," Shan's father said. As he walked around the barn the others followed.

"It's a snake track all right," Mick said. "There it goes over the soft garden ground."

Silently they all began to follow the single mark Old Ben had left. It curved in and out and it went in the direction of the hog lot. In the distance the hogs were squealing and grunting. A terrible fear seized Shan.

"He must have come out the wrong side of the barn," his father said. "I don't know how he got so confused."

Suddenly the trail stopped at the grass line.

"Maybe he wasn't confused. Maybe he was going away to sleep for the winter. Maybe he turned off here," Shan said.

"Maybe," his father said, "but don't count on it. He could have crossed the grass to the pen. I think it's too late to find anything but I'll look."

As he moved across the grass everybody stood and watched. Shan felt his mother put her arm around his shoulder. He tried not to listen to the noise from the hog lot.

When his father returned he said quietly, "I can't be sure."

"Old Ben is the best pet I ever had," said Shan. "I should never have taken him away from the clover field. I brought him where he had enemies."

"Black snakes have enemies in their own world, too." His father seemed to be talking to himself. Then he turned and spoke to Shan. "If he is gone, son, remember Old Ben lived a long time. And he had a good life with us."

"I still think he's gone off to find a place to sleep for the winter," Ward said.

"Ward may be right," Shan's mother said.

"And if he's gone to sleep, he may be back in the spring."

Shan brushed his hand over his face. "I'm going to keep hunting around here for tracks," he said. "Come on, Ward."

"All right, boys," Shan's father said. "Just don't count on finding Old Ben. Nature didn't mean for wild things to live with people. We were lucky to have Old Ben stay with us as long as he did."

"I know, Father," Shan said, "but I think I'll see Old Ben again. Anyway, if we hunt around the nest Ward found, we may find little black snakes. Maybe Ward and I will find two of Old Ben's children."

About the Author

Jesse Stuart (1906-1984) was one of America's best-known and best-loved writers. During his lifetime he published more than 2,000 poems, 460 short stories, and nine novels. His more than 60 published books include biography, autobiography, essays, and juvenile works as well as poetry and fiction. These books have immortalized the Kentucky hill country that inspired his writing.

Stuart also taught and lectured extensively. His teaching experience ranged from the one-room schoolhouses of his youth in Eastern Kentucky to the American University in Cairo, Egypt, and embraced years of service as school superintendent, high school teacher, and high school principal. "First, last, always," said Jesse Stuart, "I am a teacher. . . .Good teaching is forever, and the teacher is immortal."

Stuart wrote eight books for young people. About OLD BEN, the author wrote: "Please tell the artist to make the snake gentle-looking, I don't want to scare anyone. He was a real snake, and everything I said was true."

Book and cover design by Pamela Wise and the staff at Pamela Wise Graphic Design, Ashland, Ky.

Afterword

For the eighth year, the Kentucky Jaycees and the Jesse Stuart Foundation are distributing copies of a Jesse Stuart book to sixth graders throughout the state. The purpose of the 1995 Jesse Stuart Book Project is to put a copy of <u>Old Ben</u> in the hands of as many Kentucky sixth graders as possible, in the hope that the story will encourage them to read for pleasure and thus strengthen their reading skills. It will also promote interest in Kentucky history and literature.

Jesse Stuart once remarked that "If the United States can be called a body, Kentucky can be called its heart." He was speaking metaphorically, of course. But the Jaycees' work on the Jesse Stuart Book Project certainly adds another dimension to the word "heart," and also exemplifies Stuart's own statement, "No joy runs deeper than the feeling that I have helped a youth stand on his own two feet, to have courage and self-reliance and to find himself when he did not know who he was or where he was going."

If you would like to contribute to the Jesse Stuart Book Project, please send your check to The Jesse Stuart Foundation, P.O. Box 391, Ashland, Kentucky 41114. Every dollar that you contribute places a much-needed book in the hands of a Kentucky child.

Ms. Judy B. Thomas
Chairperson, Jesse Stuart Foundation